Edward E. Salisbury

Mr. William Diodate

of New Haven from 1717 to 1751 and his Italian ancestry, read before the

New Haven colony historical society, June 28, 1875

Edward E. Salisbury

Mr. William Diodate
of New Haven from 1717 to 1751 and his Italian ancestry, read before the New Haven colony historical society, June 28, 1875

ISBN/EAN: 9783337238278

Printed in Europe, USA, Canada, Australia, Japan

Cover: Foto ©Andreas Hilbeck / pixelio.de

More available books at **www.hansebooks.com**

MR. WILLIAM DIODATE

(Of New Haven from 1717 to 1751)

AND

HIS ITALIAN ANCESTRY,

READ BEFORE THE

JUNE 28, 1875,

BY

EDWARD E. SALISBURY.

Taken from the Society's Archives, by permission, for private circulation.
and printed, after revision, in April, 1876

Mr. WILLIAM DIODATE

AND

HIS ITALIAN ANCESTRY.

When, in the year 1821, it had been decided to oblit-
erate from the Public Square all traces of the ancient
burial-ground of New Haven, among the monuments
removed to the Cemetery on Grove street. which had
been in use since 1796, were those, as a cotemporaneous
document' informs us. of Mr. William Diodate and his
relict Sarah. Had this Society then existed. it is hardly
to be doubted that the antiquarian spirit would have
jealously guarded the old enclosure as a perpetual monument to the fathers of New Haven; in which case the
grave of William Diodate would not have been, as it now
is, an unmarked spot beneath the sod : and his descendants of the present generation would have had a locality
about which to gather a long line of associations with the
past, lately brought to light, of great interest to themselves, and not unworthy, it is thought, to be added to
the mass of early New England family-history, now being
accumulated for public as well as private ends. To pre-
serve the memory of these interesting facts, now to be
connected with this name, hitherto undistinguished—car-
rying us back, through England and Switzerland, to the
Italy of the Middle Ages—the following paper has been
prepared.

It will be proper, especially before this Society, to begin with bringing together a few items from New Haven records, respecting William Diodate himself, for which we are indebted to the researches of our honored associate Henry White. The first notice of William Diodate, in our town-records, is in 1717, when a deed of land to him, dated April 23, 1717, is recorded. On the 4th of March, 1719-20, he purchased half an acre on the corner of Elm and Church streets, where "the blue meeting house" afterwards stood—which he sold Jan. 7, 1720-1. He was married Feb. 16, 1720-1, to Sarah Dunbar, daughter of John Dunbar of New Haven, by his first wife, whose name is unknown; and in the month of May following he purchased his home-lot, on State street, on the south-west corner of what is now Court street, containing 1¼ acre, with a house and a small barn on it, for £100. In 1728-9, Feb. 24, he purchased a vacant lot adjoining, next south, containing 1¾ acre for £75; and about the year 1735 several tracts of outlands were added to his real estate. His will, dated May 26, 1747, with a codicil dated March 9, 1748-9, was proved on the 13th of May, 1751, in which year, therefore, he probably died; for, though the grave-stone of his "relict" Sarah, who survived him several years, still exists,[*] his own has not been found, so that the exact date of his death is not ascertained. So much as an outline of what the town-records tell us with regard to our subject. From the records of the First Church of New Haven we also learn that he made profession of his Christian faith on the 20th of March, 1735, under the ministry of Rev. Joseph Noyes; and that his wife had joined the same church more than twenty years before, on the 16th of April, 1713, several years before her marriage; a tankard which, till within a

short time, made part of the communion-service of plate
owned by the First Church, was her gift, and bore her
name.³ The preamble to William Diodate's will gives further indication of his religious character in these words,
which can scarcely be regarded as merely conventional:
"In the name of God, Amen: I, William Diodate of
New Haven Town and County and Colony of Connecticut in New England, do make, ordain and constitute
this my last Will and Testament: and first of all I give
and recommend my soul to God who gave it, hoping
for pardon and acceptance thro' Jesus Christ, my only
Saviour, and my body to yᵉ earth by decent Christian burial, at the discretion of my executor hereinafter
named, hoping for a glorious resurrection of the same
at the last day by the mighty power of God." We
notice, also, that, for the possible event of a failure of
heirs born to his daughter, his only child, or to her
husband, the testator directs that, after the death of his
wife, his real estate shall be divided equally between
the First Church in New Haven and the First Church
in Lyme.

Another item of interest in this will and the inventory
connected with it, is the following: "Item—all such books
as I shall die possessed off, which shall have the following
Lattin words wrote in them with my own hand-writing.
viz: 'Usque quo, Domine,' I give and devise unto my
said son-in-law Mr. Stephen Johnson, to use and improve
during his natural life, and at his death I give and devise
yᵉ same to my grandson Diodate Johnson, to be at his
dispose forever." Seventy-six volumes, mostly theological works, were thus bequeathed, valued at £20.6.7—
certainly, in themselves, a remarkable collection of books
for that time, fitted to awaken curiosity respecting its

possible origin; and this the more when one notices, by
the inventory, that among these volumes were "Mr.
Diodate's Annotations," and "Le Mercier's History of
Geneva."* Could it be, one might ask, that the author of
those Annotations, the celebrated divine of Geneva, of
the time of the Reformation, was a relative of our New
Haven testator of the same name? and did William
Diodate, one might further inquire, make an heirloom of
his library, as the words of his will imply, not only on
account of its being so rarely large for a hundred and
twenty-five years ago, but also on account of family-asso-
ciations with it, perhaps as having come down to himself,
in part at least, from that learned divine? and was the
significant motto, written by him in each volume, a me-
morial of those times of conflict and peril in which the
theologian Diodati of Geneva had lived, and patiently
wrought out his life-work, there under the shadow of the
icy Mt. Blanc, shut out from the sunny land of Italian
forefathers? An affirmative answer to the first of these
inquiries, which suggested itself, indeed, some time since,
to one of the descendants of our William Diodate, but
which we are now first able to make on satisfactory
grounds, almost inevitably leads to the same reply to all
of them.

The inventory of William Diodate also shows, as having
belonged to his estate, a considerable amount of gold and
silver coin, or bonds and notes for the same, besides sil-
ver-plate; which accords with what we otherwise know,
by tradition, that he dealt in coin and plate, as at once
a banker and broker, and a trader in the various articles
of gold and silver which were in use at the time. Not
improbably, therefore, the communion-tankard, marked
with his wife's name, came from his own establishment.

Family-tradition says that he had "the first store in New Haven"—whatever that may mean, as applied to the early part of the 18th century.

It is to be noticed, further, that his residence in the colony of Connecticut must have dated from a yet earlier period than that of the first appearance of his name on the town-records of New Haven; for a copy of Dr. Diodati's Annotations, presented to the Collegiate School at Saybrook in 1715, was his gift: possibly, he may have been drawn to New Haven by a hereditary appreciation of academic learning, as well as by the new business-life growing out of the first establishment of the college here; the very year in which he is first heard of in New Haven was that of the removal of the Collegiate School from Saybrook, and its beginning here, to be known—from the next year onward—as Yale College.

Crossing, now, to the shores of England, whither the personal history of this old New Havener carries us, we take with us, as our chief thread of connection, some records, still existing in a Bible which belonged to William Diodate in the year 1728, in his own hand-writing, which inform us that his father's name was John, and his mother the eldest daughter of John Morton, Esq., by Elizabeth, only child of John Wicker, and the widow of Alderman Cranne (as we read) of London; and that he had a brother John, older than himself, and a sister Elizabeth.[5] In addition to these records, we have the accepted family-tradition that, after having been in America for some years, without communication with his relatives in the old country, he at length went back, and found his father and brother had died, and that he himself had been supposed to be dead, so that his claims to property, as a member of the family, were set aside; whereupon

he accepted from his sister, by way of compromise, an
offer "to supply his store in New Haven with goods
as long as she lived," which she did, not only during
his lifetime, but afterwards, while his widow lived, who
continued the business; and we also have the will of
the sister, under her married name of Elizabeth Scarlett,
dated Feb. 23, 1768, in which the principal bequests are
to the daughter of her deceased brother in New England
and her children. These materials for tracing the ancestry of our subject were put, last year, into the hands of
the distinguished American antiquary Col. Joseph L.
Chester, long resident in London; who received them
with interest, and added to them others, of great value,
from wills and letters of administration recorded in Doctors' Commons, and from the records of several London
Parishes, etc.

Meanwhile, recourse was had, also, to a branch of the
Diodati family still residing in Geneva, through the kind
intervention of Rev. Leonard W. Bacon, now for some
time a sojourner in that city—which led to the discovery
of a large mass of most interesting family-papers, distinctly
showing the Diodatis to have been an old Italian family,
tracing back their history to Lucca, in the Middle Ages,
and marking the race as one of high rank, in all its generations, with so many individual names of distinction
belonging to it as have rarely appertained to a single
family; preserving, too, in honor, the memory of an English offset, though without knowledge of the American
branch. We owe the privilege of using these papers
chiefly to Mr. Gabriel C. Diodati of Geneva, who has
most courteously met and furthered the inquiries of our
friend Mr. Bacon, besides assisting us otherwise. This
friend has also sent us a Life of John Diodati (Vie de

Jean Diodati, Théologien Génevois, 1576-1649) by E. de Budé, Lausanne, 1869—from which we have derived further aid in tracing William Diodate's descent. We have drawn, also, from a Dutch monograph: Jean Diodati, door Dr. G. D. J. Schotel, 's Gravenhage, 1844, to which De Budé refers for details, which is, evidently, the basis of his own publication, and for which the author had the use of family-papers. David L. Gardiner, Esq., connected with the Diodati family by marriage, who just now resides in Geneva, has also aided our investigations.

Our information from all sources harmonizes so satisfactorily that no essential fact would seem to be wanting. But the settlement of the nearer ancestry of our subject is mainly due to a happy combination suggested by Col. Chester.

The most ancient records of the Diodatis tell us that the first of their race who settled in Lucca, Cornelio by name, came there from Coreglia in the year 1300.[1] Whether he came as a nobleman, or, according to the middle-age conception of nobility, as a landed proprietor, to throw the weight of his influence on that side, in the great strife for power in the Italian cities, between those who held the soil and those whose claims to consideration were based only on the possession of wealth acquired by commerce, we are not informed. But, inasmuch as within the last twenty years of the 13th century, according to Sismondi,[2] that strife for power had ended with the absolute exclusion of the nobility from all control in the republics of Italy ; and as we find the representative of the fourth generation of Diodatis in Lucca, named Michele, to have been an Ancient, four times Gonfalonier, and a Decemvir in 1370 (the

very year of a revival of popular liberty in Lucca, after
fifty-six years of servitude through the prevalence of the
Ghibelline party), while his father, Alessandro, seems to be
remembered only as a physician—the probability is that
what led to the original settlement of the family in
Lucca was no ambition to assert prescriptive right, but
rather that new sense of widening opportunity for the
improvement of one's condition and culture, which then
animated Italian city-life, and was destined, under the
favoring circumstances of the age, to bring upon the
theatre of history all those names which have added
most to the glory of Italy in art and learning.

The year 1300, indeed, is memorable not only as marking an important political and social crisis, but as a note-
worthy epoch in the history of Italian architecture,
painting and poetry. From 1294 to 1300, the year in
which he died, Arnolfo was directing the construction of
the Santa Maria del Fiore, the cathedral-church of Flor-
ence, of which the dome was afterwards completed by
Brunelleschi ; about the year 1300, Andrea Pisano was at
work on his gates of the Baptistery of Pisa ; Giotto, too,
was passing from his shepherd-life, to carry into the art of
painting a new inspiration derived from converse with
simple nature ; and that same year was the time when
Dante imagined himself to have voyaged through the
regions of the dead, transferring thither friendships and
affections, but more often enmities and bitter judgments,
of earth, in his impassioned, soul-stirring descriptions of
purifying pains, or hopeless agonies, or seraphic bliss, of
the departed. Evidently, the age was pre-eminent for intellectual movement ; and it is not a little interesting to
associate with this movement, as we so naturally may, the
coming in of our Diodatis to take part in the city-life

of Lucca, who were, in generations to come, not only there but in foreign lands, to prove themselves an eminently stirring race, by public services, literary, professional, civil, military, and diplomatic, in eminent positions in State and Church, almost always on the side of liberty and truth.

Passing over the son of the Decemvir of 1370, Dr. Nicolò Diodati, who died in 1442, we come to a generation of fifteen children of his, by marriage with Francesca di Poggio, among whom the third by birth, named Michele, born in 1410, who married Caterina Buonvisi, was a professor in Padua and Pisa—probably of medicine —and afterwards a physician in Lucca, where he was pensioned on 300 livres by the city : and another, Antonio, born in 1416, held the office of Ancient, and was Gonfalonier in 1461. Whether it was by influences favorable to liberty, or adverse, that these members of the family were thus distinguished, cannot be certainly told : we know, however, that for about thirty years, in the beginning of the 15th century, Lucca was under a usurper, Paolo Guinigi ; and the republics of Italy, in general, during that century, were becoming more and more aristocratic in spirit, from the fact that citizenship in them, not being a gift to be bestowed upon new comers, was handed down as a privilege belonging to certain families ; while official position must of course have become, still more, the prerogative of a favored class.·

The race seems to have been continued only through Alessandro, son of the Professor Michele, born in 1459 : his son Geronimo, born in 1465, who was an eminent literary man, and nine times Ancient, having died childless, and no descendants of his third son, Antonio, who was three times Ancient and four times Gonfalonier, being named. Alessandro was repeatedly Gonfalonier from 1494: the mother of his children was Angela Balbani, whom he married in 1510, she being then fifteen years old, and he fifty-one. Now began those encroachments upon the fair domain of liberty and culture in Italy by foreign powers, which culminated in the overthrow of Italian independence under the Emperor Charles 5th in the middle of the 16th century. But with this new political influence from beyond the Alps there came, also, the seeds of evangelical truth ; and "in the first half of the 16th century," by the blessing of God upon the zealous labors of the erudite and devout Peter Martyr Vermigli, says De Budé, "no city of Italy counted so many devoted evangelical Christians as the capital of the republic of Lucca ;"* and a reformed church was founded there, which the Diodati family was known to favor, though, apparently, without an open departure from the old fold until a somewhat later period.

In 1541, the Emperor Charles 5th and Pope Paul 3d had their memorable interview at Lucca on the affairs of Germany, the emperor being then in the mood to favor Protestantism for his own ambition's sake ; when Michele Diodati, one of several sons of the last named Alessandro, born in 1510, was Gonfalonier, and, as the family-tradition runs, lodged the emperor in his palace. Just then was born to the chief magistrate of the republic, by his wife Anna, daughter of Martino Buonvisi, his third son ; the emperor, continues the tradition of the family, stood godfather to this child, baptized by the pope, and gave him his own name, together with the lordship of two counties, and a quartering from the imperial arms, and, on his departure, left behind him for the child one of his insignia of diamonds, which he happened to be wearing about his neck."

This Carolo Diodati was sent in his youth to Lyons, to serve an apprentisage in one of the banking houses of the Buonvisi, his mother's family ; became a frequenter of the reformed preaching there, and at heart a Protestant ; but the massacre of St. Bartholomew drove him out of France, and he took refuge in Geneva, where he was tenderly received and entertained by the pastor of the church of Italian refugees, already established there, Nicolò Balbani, was admitted into the church, became a citizen of Geneva on the 29th of December, 1572, and contracted a second marriage with Marie daughter of Vincenzo Mai, by whom he had four sons, Joseph, Theodore, Jean and Samuel, and three daughters, Anne, Marie and Madeleine.

But, before we pursue the fortunes of this branch of the family, which especially interests us, on account of descendants of the name in England and America, three other lines claim our notice. First, Michele the Gonfalonier of 1541 had a brother Nicolò, born in 1512, who married Elisabeta daughter of Geronimo Arnolfini, and by her had a son, Pompeio, born in 1542, "qui Pompeius" to quote a family-document "Catholicâ pejeratâ Fide, Genevam se contulit." Pompeio was married in Italy to Laura daughter of Giuliano Calandrini, and settled at Geneva with his wife and mother in 1575," all having previously joined the reformed congregation which originated at Lucca under Peter Martyr, and having been compelled to quit their native land, with other families, by the new zeal of Pius 5th against the Reformers, in league with Philip 2d. As to the descendants of Pompeio Diodati, beside a son Eli, who became an eminent jurist, he had a son Alessandro, who was a distinguished physician, at one time physician in ordinary to Louis 13th of France, who

himself had a son Jean, and a grandson Gabriel; and in
1719 this Gabriel received from Louis 15th, " by the grace
of God, King of France and Navarre," a sort of charter
of nobility, still preserved in the family, recognizing the
Diodatis as one of the most ancient and noble families of
Lucca, which for several centuries had held the honors
and dignities peculiar to nobility, and allied itself with
noble families in Lucca and Geneva, without having ever
derogated from its dignity ; and empowering them, accordingly, to hold certain lands in the Pays de Gex, which
they could not enjoy without the royal grant. Possibly
these lands are the same, or in part the same, which, as
we shall see, had been bequeathed by a grandson of the
namesake of Charles 5th, who had died thirty-nine years
before, a bachelor, to whichever of his nephews should go
to Geneva to live : neither of them having fulfilled this
condition, and his will not having provided for the case,
the bequest lapsed ; and a royal grant may have been,
consequently, applied for in favor of a collateral branch
of the family.   In the latter half of the last century, however, a lineal descendant of one of those nephews built
the castle of Vernier, in the bailiwick of Gex—probably,
therefore, on the Gex estate of the Diodatis—which, at
his death, was sold, and soon after passed, by a second
sale, to the Naville family, who hold it now. The builder
of the Diodati villa, a little way up lake Leman from
Geneva, which was occupied by Lord Byron, and is still
in the family, was a Gabriel Diodati, probably the same
who received this grant from Louis 15th. The line of
direct descent from Pompeio Diodati came to an end, by
the death of Count Jean Diodati, in 1807.

Next is to be noted, that Pompeio Diodati had a brother
Nicolò, who, in the family-records, appears as having

attained to high dignities under the new order of things in Italy (though at one time, apparently, an emigrant to Geneva for religion's sake),[1] and had, beside many other children, two sons Giovanni and Giulio, of whom the former became a Knight Templar and Prior of Venice, and the latter a "Summus Copiarum Præfectus," or Major General, of the Emperor Ferdinand 2d, the Catholic, the leader of the Catholic party in the beginning of the Thirty Years' War, as appears from the inscription on a monument in the Church of St. Augustine in Lucca.[2] This branch of the family, also, is now extinct.

Another branch of the family which retained its hold upon the old home in Italy, and possessed a long inheritance of worldly honors, came of Ottaviano Diodati, a brother of the namesake of the Emperor Charles 5th, born in 1555, who married, at Genoa, Eleonora di Casa Nuova. He himself was Gonfalonier in 1620; his son, Lorenzo, held the same dignity in 1651; his grandson Ottaviano, in 1669; his great-grandson Lorenzo was repeatedly Gonfalonier and minister to various European courts; his great-great-grandson Ottaviano, having been, first, in holy orders, was afterwards Senator and Ancient; and the son of this last Ottaviano, another Lorenzo, was " Præfectus Militum," or General, to Charles 3d of Spain, whose reign covered the years from 1759 to 1788. During the sixteenth century the republic of Lucca still maintained its independence, but under a republican form of government aristocracy ruled; the seventeenth century, under the malign influence of Spanish absolutism, was a time of universal moral, intellectual and political death to Italy, which Lucca could not escape by attempting, as it did, to hide itself from observation under an enforced silence, with a law forbidding the publication of any facts of its history ; and the same reserve and withdrawal from all active concern for the national honor, was even more marked as the eighteenth century came and passed." Such are the historical facts in the light of which the honors of the Diodatis during this period are to be interpreted. The generalship under Charles 3d of Spain is also significant, as showing that one of the family, at that time, was ready to sacrifice even what little remained of the life of his country to the will of the alien oppressor. The second Lorenzo of this branch had also, already, allied himself with Spain, for his wife was Isabella daughter of a noble Catalan named Bellet. In this connection may be mentioned, further, that "there is in the possession of the family [in Geneva] a superb folio, bound in crimson velvet, of fourteen pages of vellum, with the imperial seal of Joseph 2d [1765-90] hanging from it in a gilt box, which recites the dignities of the Diodati family in magnificent terms, and confirms to it the title of Count of the Empire. One of the pages is occupied with a fine illumination of the family-arms, the shield being placed on the imperial eagle.'"

Returning, now, to take up the thread of our story where we dropped it, at the mention of the names of the children of Carolo Diodati, the namesake of the Emperor Charles 5th—as to his daughters, they allied themselves, severally, with the families Burlamaqui, Offredi and Pellissari, all doubtless fellow-exiles with the Diodatis; and that is all we know of the female line of Carolo's posterity. Of the sons we are told of the fortunes of only two, Theodore and Jean. Theodore Diodati, born in 1574 at Geneva, being educated as a physician, went early to England, where he is heard of, says Professor Masson, in his introduction to Milton's Latin Elegies, "as living, about the

year 1609, near Brentford, in professional attendance on
Prince Henry, and the Princess Elizabeth [afterwards
Queen of Bohemia]."" He received the degree of Doctor of Medicine at Leyden, Oct. 6, 1615, and was admitted
a Licentiate of the Royal College of Physicians in London, Jan. 24, 1616-17. He became an eminent practitioner,
"much among persons of rank," residing in London,
apparently, to the age of seventy-six, his burial having
been in the parish-church of St. Bartholomew the Less,
Feb. 12, 1650–1. "The naturalized London physician,"
says Masson, "is to be fancied, it seems, as a cheery, active
veteran, with courtly and gallant Italian ways to the
last."" He was twice married, first to an English "lady of
good birth and fortune," by whom he had three children ;
and afterwards to another English lady, who brought him
"goods and estate," survived him, and was his executrix.
The children of Dr. Diodati were Philadelphia, buried at
St. Anne's, Blackfriars, Aug. 10, 1638; John, "mentioned,"
as Col. Chester says, "in the will of Elizabeth Cundall
(widow of Henry Cundall, the partner of Burbage in the
Globe Theatre), dated September, 1635 :" and Charles,
the well-known youthful companion and bosom-friend of
Milton, whose life and character are delineated, in connection with those of Milton, in so very interesting a
manner, by means of the joint researches of Professor
Masson and Col. Chester, in the former's Life of
Milton and in his edition of Milton's Poetical Works ;
to whom Milton addressed two of his Latin sonnets,
and who was the subject of his Epitaphium Damonis.
Specially note-worthy, in the relations of the two friends,
is the contrast between Milton's studious gravity and the
blithesome cheerfulness of Diodati, whom "one fancies,"
says Masson, "as a quick, amiable, intelligent youth, with

something of his Italian descent visible in his face and manner."⁕ This Charles "was born about 1609," says Col. Chester, "as he was matriculated at Oxford, from Trinity College, Feb. 7, 1622–3, aged thirteen at his last birth-day ;" and to the same diligent antiquary we owe the discovery of the date of his death, in Aug., 1638, his burial having been at St. Anne's, Blackfriars, Aug. 27, 1638, only seventeen days after that of his sister. "Letters of administration on his estate, in which he is described as a bachelor, were granted to his brother John in the Prerogative Court of Canterbury, Oct. 3, 1638." John (grandfather of our William), the brother of Charles, was married at St. Margaret's, Westminster, July 28, 1635, to Isabel Underwood, who died and was buried in June, 1638, leaving a son Richard, who was baptized June 29 of the same year. Philadelphia and Charles, though unmarried at the time of their death, were not living with their father, but, as Col. Chester has shown, at a "Mr. Dollam's" in Blackfriars ; which is explained by the supposition of a family-feud consequent upon the second marriage of their father, a fact plainly enough alluded to, indeed, in one of the Latin letters of Milton, addressed to his friend in 1637 : "quod, nisi bellum hoc novercale vel Dacico vel Sarmatico infestius sit, debebis profecto maturare, ut ad nos saltem in hyberna concedas."⁕ Nor is there any child, or grandchild, named in the will of the old physician, who makes a nephew Theodore his residuary legatee ; so that either all his direct descendants had died before him, or he carried the family-quarrel with him to his grave ; and the latter appears to be the fact. In England, it may be well to mention, the family-name was variously corrupted, being written as Deodate, Dyodat and Diodate, which last is the American form.

Another son of the namesake of Charles 5th was the Rev. Jean Diodati, born in Geneva in 1576, whose home was in that city during the whole of his life of seventy-three years, but whose fame and influence were all over Europe while he lived, and of a nature not to perish with the lapse of time, like those honors which fell, as we have seen, to others of his race. The main points in his life, and his principal works, have been often noticed; yet with less of living portraiture of character than could be desired, except in the recent publication of De Budé, of which the title has been already given, which we shall chiefly follow, therefore, in the sketch here given. From his youth, when he already manifested great acuteness of mind and precision of judgment, he was destined for the sacred ministry. His education was in the Academy of Geneva, under such men as Beza and Casaubon, and so rapid was his progress that he became a doctor of theology before the age of nineteen, and soon after succeeded Casaubon as professor of Hebrew, and in the old age of Beza assisted to fill his place. Already in the year 1603, when he was only twenty-seven years old, he presented to the Venerable Company of Pastors of Geneva his Italian version of the Bible, a work which was highly esteemed by his most learned contemporaries, and has never yet been superseded. The following is an extract from a letter of Isaac Casaubon acknowledging a copy from the translator : " Lorsque récemment j'ai répondu à ta lettre amicale, illustre Deodati, je n'avais pas encore reçu le présent vraiment divin dont tu m'as gratifié. Aussi t'en ai-je remercié davance, en homme qui ne l'avait pas lu, et qui n'avait pas assouvi par une lecture approfondie la soif d'en jouir comme j'ai taché de le faire plus tard . . . En effet, très savant homme, dès que j'eus jeté les yeux sur ta version et les

notes si remarquables, je fus tellement intéressé que je
resolus sur le champ de prendre connaissance de tout
l'ouvrage avec le plus grand soin. . . . . . Maintenant
comme d'autres soucis assez différents m'écrasent pour
ainsi dire, ce sera plus lentement mais plus attentivement
que je poursuivrai la lecture que j'ai commencée, et je
le ferai avec d'autant plus de persévérance que déjà sou-
vent j'ai éprouvé quel grand profit je trouverai dans
l'étude de ta version et de tes notes."[20]

But Jean Diodati was far from being a man of learning
alone : he had too much of Italian fervor of temperament,
and was too deeply imbued with the Christian spirit, not
to wish to take a part in spreading the faith which he
could not but nourish by the study of the Scriptures ; and
his attention was most naturally directed, in a special
manner, to his beloved native land.   Venice was the out-
post which he aspired to take possession of for the cause
of Reform, where a great hostility to the Papal See, in
consequence of the excommunication of the Republic by
Paul 5th, the potent influence, though secret, of the celebrated Fra Paolo Sarpi, the encouragement of the English
ambassador Wotton, and other circumstances, seemed to
have opened the way.   More or less, during the years
from 1605 to 1610, our Diodati was engaged in this enterprise, and in that time he twice visited Venice in person.
His plans, however, failed, and we refer to the undertak-
ing more for the light it throws upon the character of
the man than for any historical importance attaching to
it.   Between himself and Sarpi (of whom he says, evidently with impatience, that his "incomparable learning
was diluted by such a scrupulous prudence, and so little
enlivened and sharpened by fervor of spirit, although accompanied by a very upright and wholly exemplary life,"

that he judged him incapable of any boldness of action, to effect an entrance for the truth), there would appear to have been little affinity of spirit. Yet his enterprise and courage were not the fruit of inconsiderate self-confidence. " I shall be very careful," he wrote to Du Plessis Mornay, in France, with respect to his plans for Venice, "not to oppose a barrier to the very free operation of the Divine Spirit, either by the consideration of my own incapacity, or by apprehension of any danger. I am sure that God, who beyond my hopes and aspirations used me in the matter of His Scriptures, so opportunely for this great work, with happy success, as the judgments of diverse distinguished persons, and your own among others, lead me to believe, will also give me a mouth, and power and wisdom, if need be, to serve in these parts for the advancement of His kingdom, and the destruction of great Babylon."

On his return for the last time from Venice, Jean Diodati was first formally consecrated to the ministry of the Word, for which, there is reason to believe, he was especially fitted. " His eloquent voice," it has been said, " his impressive delivery, and his profound convictions, produced such an effect on his numerous hearers that they were strengthened in their belief, corrected in their conduct, renovated in their sentiments." But let us hear, on the other hand, with what genuine modesty he assumed the solemn responsibility of a preacher. "On my return," he writes to Du Plessis Mornay, " I was on a sudden charged with the sacred ministry, to which I had engaged myself by promise before my departure, and not without many apprehensions and much awe, which kept me in a state of great perplexity until I resolved to abandon myself, aside from and contrary to all reasoning and judgment of my own, to the necessity of the case, and the call of God, which, as it

has respect to the needs of His church, will, I hope and
am already confident, be accompanied with His powerful
benediction, so that I may in some small measure answer
to the same." So well did he meet this call that several
churches of France, in the course of time, sought him
for their pastor, and Prince Maurice, at the time of the
Synod of Dort, pressed him to remain in the Low
Countries; but he never settled himself long out of
Geneva. Some want of clearness in discourse has been
charged to Diodati, which he was ready to justify by say-
ing, on one occasion, "Clear waters are never deep;" and
his fervor seems to have sometimes become vehemence.
As a preacher, he was ever distinguished by a noble boldness, which Innocent 10th is said to have felt the force of,
to his own correction, on the report of a sermon of Diodati, in which he had declared the Church of Rome to be
scandalously governed by a woman, meaning Donna
Olympia. "From Morrice's 'State Letters of the Rt.
Hon. the earl of Orrery,'" says Chalmers, "we learn that,
when invited to preach at Venice, he was obliged to
equip himself in a trooper's habit, a scarlet cloak with a
sword, and in that garb he mounted the pulpit; but was
obliged to escape again to Geneva, from the wrath of a
Venetian nobleman, whose mistress, affected by one of
Diodati's sermons, had refused to continue her connection with her keeper."

After the death of Henry 4th, when there were fears
of an attack upon Geneva by the Duke of Savoy, he was
appointed to visit the Protestants of France in behalf of
his native city; and his mission was highly successful.

One of the chief marks of distinction received by our
Genevese divine, and which is next to be noticed in the
order of time, was his appointment, jointly with Tronchin,

to represent Geneva at the Synod of Dort, in 1618 19; and here he comes before us in a somewhat new light. There had been doubt about inviting any delegates from the chief seat of Calvinistic doctrine, to avoid an appearance of partiality, in calling them to take part in judging of the orthodoxy of the Remonstrants; nor could there have been chosen two men less disposed to any compromise in matters of theological opinion, apparently, than our Diodati and his colleague. Neither that tenderness of sympathy for errorists, nor that broader mental habit of discrimination between the essential and the unessential, which we have reason to suppose belonged to Diodati by nature and through the influence of his special training in Biblical study, seems to have preserved him from a certain hardness of resistance to the plea for toleration, or at least for a liberal and charitable judgment, without prejudice, of those who could not conscientiously swear by Calvin. Our authority on this subject is Brandt's History of the Reformation and other Ecclesiastical Transactions in and about the Low Countries, vol. 3d of the English translation, which, though from the side of the Remonstrant party, is relied upon for its statement of facts. In an early session of the Synod, on the question of its right to adjudicate, raised by the Remonstrants, both the Genevese deputies declared " that, if people obstinately refused to submit to the lawful determinations of the Church, then there remained two methods to be used against them : the one was that the civil magistrate might stretch out his arm of compulsion ; and the other, that the Church might exert her power in order to separate and to cut off, by a public sentence, those who violated the laws of God." What more absolute control over opinion was ever asserted even by the See of Rome ! Later, as we read, " Diodatus said,

in the name of those of Geneva, that the doctrines of the
Remonstrants might be sufficiently learned from the con-
ference at the Hague and their books. Let them go, then,
said he, as unworthy to appear any longer at the Synod.
There was no difficulty in coming at the knowledge of
their doctrines without them, and even against their will."
Yet, at the 106th session, it is said, " Diodatus, whose turn
of haranguing in publick had been now superseded several
times, on account of his indisposition, treated about the
perseverance of the saints," . . . and "spoke of the
doctrine of reprobation in milder terms than the Contra-
remonstrants were wont to do, denying that sin was a
fruit of reprobation. When he came to the Remonstrant
arguments, relating to their opinion of perseverance," the
record adds, "he was heard to say, 'that he was not prepared to answer the evasions and exceptions of those new
philosophers, who by their subtilties and niceties over-
turned all principles, and brought all things into doubt; as
for him, he would keep to his good old ways.'" At the
121st session, when the opinions of several of the foreign
divines were taken on the article in the statement of the
Remonstrants relative to perseverance, "those of Geneva
said, 'that they obscured the honour of God; that they
sapped the foundations of salvation; that they robbed
men of all their comfort; that they brought in rank popery
again, and cooked up the old Pelagian heresy again with
a new sauce; they therefore prayed to God with all
their hearts, that the supreme powers of this land would
exert themselves courageously and piously, in order to
extirpate this corrupt leven, and to free all their churches
from the dangers of this contagion.'"

When the time came to draw up canons which should
express the decisions of this specially Calvinistic synod,

Jean Diodati was one of six deputies chosen to act with
the President for that purpose; and meanwhile his voice
was given in favor of a "personal censure" pronounced
upon those whose opinions were condemned, "as intro-
ducers of novelties, disturbers of their country, and of the
Netherland churches; as obstinate and disobedient pro-
moters of factions and preachers of errors; as guilty and
convicted of corrupting religion, of schism, or dissolving
the unity of the Church, and of having given very grievous
scandal and offense; for all which they were sentenced to
be deprived of all ecclesiastical and academical offices.'"

From Dort, Diodati went to England, doubtless, in part,
to visit his brother Theodore.

Beside his Italian version of the Scriptures, Jean Diodati also made a French translation, from his Italian, the
publication of which, though discouraged for years, was
finally permitted in 1644: and he is said to have under-
taken, to what end does not appear, a version in Latin;
the family-archives also intimate that a Spanish version
was due to him, though it is hardly to be believed that
this could have been more than a translation, by some
other hand, of his so highly reputed Italian.

In 1621, there appeared at Geneva a French translation,
by Diodati, of a History of the Council of Trent, written
in Italian, in the interest of Protestantism, and ascribed
to Fra Paolo Sarpi. He also translated the Psalms into
"rime vulgare Italiane," published at Geneva in 1608;
and was the author of Annotationes in Biblia, published
there in 1607, substantially the same with the notes which
Casaubon speaks of in his letter above quoted, and with
the notes which accompany his French version; a later
edition appeared in 1644, under the title of Glossae in
Sancta Biblia. Other valuable works, and many single

dissertations on various theological and ecclesiastical sub-
jects, which it is needless to specify here, were also written
by him. There is reason to believe, however, that the
chief occupation of the last third of Diodati's life, beside
his duties of instruction in the Academy of Geneva, was
the revision and re-casting of his notes on the Scriptures,
in connection with his translations. From Masson we
learn, further, that "besides his celebrity as professor of
theology, city preacher, translator of the Bible into Italian, and author of several theological works, Diodati was
celebrated as an instructor of young men of rank sent to
board in his house. About the year 1639," he adds, "there
were many young foreigners of distinction pursuing their
studies in Geneva, including Charles Gustavus, afterwards
king of Sweden, and several princes of German Protestant houses, and some of these appear to have been among
Diodati's private pupils."[31] We only mention further, as
included in this period, that Milton in 1639, on his return
from Italy, to use his own words, was "daily in the society of John Diodati, the most learned professor of theology,"[32] from whom he probably first heard of the death
of his friend Charles, the nephew of the divine. The
death of the Rev. Jean Diodati occurred in 1649.

This distinguished divine married Madeleine daughter
of Michel Burlamaqui,[33] at Geneva, in Dec., 1600; by
whom he had nine children, five sons and four daughters.
Of the sons, who alone concern us here, one was Theodore, made Doctor of Medicine at Leyden, Feb. 4, 1643,
and admitted Honorary Member of the Royal College of
Physicians of London in Dec., 1664; who resided in London, though not, as it seems, in the practice of his profession, but as a merchant: in the letters of administration
on his estate, granted July 24, 1680, he is called " Doctor

in Medicine and Merchant." He had no children, and bequeathed most of his property—including two estates " in the bailiwick of Gex, one in the village and parish of Fernex, the other in the village and parish of Vernier, within a league of Geneva "—reserving a life-interest in the real estate to a sister Renée—to three nephews named Philip, John and Ralph; with these provisos, however: that "if either revolt from the Reformed Religion in which he was brought up, I disinherit him," and "if all said nephews die without issue, then my estate to go to build a hospital for poor strangers at Geneva." The real estate was to pass, eventually, to whichever one of his nephews should go to Geneva to live, of whom he mentions Ralph as most likely so to do; and the property must not be sold, but kept in the family. We also find the following item in his will: " There is also at Geneva, in my sister Renée Diodati her keeping, a copy of the French Bible of the translation of my deceased father, reviewed and enlarged by him with divers annotations, since the former copy which was printed before his death, which I doe esteeme very much, and I will that it be printed, etc." Legacies were also left to the poor of the French and Italian churches of Geneva, the French churches of London and the Savoy, and the Italian church of London, and those of Fernex and Vernier. Another son of the Rev. Jean Diodati was Charles, who also went to England, on whose estate, on the 13th of Aug., 1651, letters of administration were granted "to Theodore Diodati next of kin "—evidently his brother Theodore—styling him " of St. Mary Magdalen, Old Fish Street, London, bachelor." A third son, named Samuel, " became a merchant in Holland," whither he went in 1658; he lived single and died in 1676. Another son was named Marc, who also died without descendants, in 1641, at Amsterdam.

The only son through whom the line of direct descent from the Genevese divine was perpetuated, was Philippe, who studied theology, first under his father and other learned professors of Geneva, and afterwards at Montauban in France ; went to Holland, and was in 1651 installed pastor of the Walloon Church of Leyden. He married Elizabeth daughter of Sébastien Francken, alderman of Dort and counsellor of the Provincial Court of Holland ; with whom he lived a happy married life of five years, and died Oct. 6, 1659. Four sons were born to him, of whom one died in infancy, and the other three were Philippe Sébastien, Rodolphe and Jean, the three nephews of the Theodore just named, whom he made, as we have seen, his principal legatees. Philippe settled in Holland ; he administered, however, in England, in 1680, on his uncle Theodore's estate, with his brother Jean. In the record of Doctors' Commons he is called Doctor of Laws. He married Lidia Blankart, and was a counsellor at Rotterdam. Ralph, or Rudolphe, it seems, did not go to Geneva to live, as his uncle expected : he went to the East ; married on the Mauritius Catherine Saaijmans of that island ; was at one time Chief of the Dutch East India Company in Japan ; and died at Batavia.

The only other son of Philippe Diodati was Jean, born at Leyden July 28, 1658, who, after passing a commercial apprentisage at Dort, embarked for Batavia in the island of Java, in May, 1679, to establish himself as a merchant there. On the 2d of April, 1680—probably, therefore, in India—he married Aldegonda Trouvers (Travers ?), of a prominent Irish family, as is said, by whom he had several children ; and died in 1711 at Surat, where his remains are said to have reposed beneath a "superb monument," erected to his memory by his daughters." His wife had died in 1698.

Two of the children of Jean Diodati by Aldegonda Trouvers were Philippe and Salomon, born at Dort in 1686 and 1688, who both became associates of the Dutch East India Company at Batavia. The former died childless, at Batavia, on the 26th of Jan., 1733, bequeathing 75,000 francs to the Cathedral of Dort, for the purchase of communion-plate. The latter, on the 7th of December, 1713, married Gertrude daughter of Jerome Slott, and in 1733 returned to Holland with his wife and two sons, Martin Jacob and Antoine Josué, and settled at the Hague, where he died in 1753. Of these two sons, Martin established himself in Holland, and died without male descendants; the other, born in 1728, having studied theology at Geneva, went back to the Hague, and became chaplain to the King of Holland. Later, he married Marie Aimée Rilliet of Geneva, and settled there. He was the builder of the castle of Vernier, already referred to (p. 14), and lived there till he died, in 1791. He was a great amateur of the fine arts, and had his house always full of artists; and, in consequence of his expensive style of living, left his fortune very much diminished to his children, of whom he had eight, three sons and five daughters. But the name was transmitted by only one of the sons, named Jacques Amédée, whose son Edouard, professor in the Academy of Geneva and Librarian of that city, was the father of Mr. Gabriel C. Diodati and his two brothers, Messieurs Theodore and Aloys, who worthily maintain the honors of the family at Geneva at the present time.

We have thus briefly sketched the history of this remarkable family; and all of the name appearing in English records have been mentioned in their places in the line of descent, down to and including the grandfather of William Diodate ; unless a separate place could have been found for a John Diodati, who engaged in business in London, being called a " Factor " in some entries concerning him, and on whose estate letters of administration were granted Feb. 25, 1687-8, to his son John, his relict Sarah renouncing. But this person is identified by Col. Chester, after thorough research, with John the brother of Milton's friend, who buried his wife Isabel Underwood in 1638, as stated above (p. 18), a son of his by a second marriage being the father of William. The identification is made necessary by the proved impossibility of finding any other place for John the " Factor " in the pedigree : while the date of the birth of William's father corresponds with all the known dates of this John's life, supposing him one with the brother of Milton's friend of the same name.

All that English records tell us of William Diodate's father is embraced in the following particulars. On the 14th of May, 1682, a license was given him to marry Mercy Tilney, of St. Michael Bassishaw, London, being himself described, in the marriage-license, as a " bachelor, aged about 22 [therefore born about 1660], with parents' consent :" and by this marriage he had four children, who all died in infancy. The wife died in the parish of St. Andrew, Undershaft, London, and was buried at Blackfriars, Sept. 18, 1689. On the 6th of Jan., 1689 90, he had a license to marry Mistress Elizabeth Morton, of Tottenham, County Middlesex, he being then described as " of St. Andrew, Undershaft, London, merchant, widower, aged about 30." The history of Elizabeth Morton, worked out by Col. Chester with much care and labor, is given by him in brief, as follows : " Rev. Adrian Whicker, vicar of Kirtlington, Oxfordshire (where he was buried 16 June, 1616), by his wife Jane (buried there 8 Dec., 1641), had several children, of whom the eldest son was John Whicker, born in St. Aldate's parish in the city of Oxford, who became a merchant in London, but at his death desired to be buried at Kirtlington. His will, dated 8 Sept., 1660, was proved 12 Feb., 1660-1. By his wife Jane, who was buried at St. Olave, Hart street, London, Mar. 1, 1637-8, he had five daughters, of whom three only survived. The second daughter, Elizabeth Whicker, was baptized at St. Olave, Hart street, 21 Aug., 1623. She first married Richard Crandley, Alderman of London, who was buried at St. Olave, Hart street, 12 Dec., 1655. From his will it is evident that they had no children. She remarried John Morton at St. Olave, Hart street, in July, 1658, and a female child (unnamed) was buried there 5 July, 1659. They had also a son John Whicker Morton, who married Elizabeth Medlicott, and died 18 May, 1693, and was buried at Tackley in Oxfordshire; and also a daughter Theodosia, who was her father's executrix, and then un-married. Their only other daughter was Elizabeth, who married John Diodati." The general coincidence of these results of a search in English records respecting the Morton-marriage of John Diodati, with the facts already stated as derived from William Diodate's Bible, will not fail to be noticed. But that statement is further dupli-cated by what we learn in England with regard to the children born of this Morton-marriage, who are there seen to have been three in number, namely, John, William and Elizabeth. John, son of John and Elizabeth Dio-dati, was matriculated at Oxford, from Balliol College, April 6, 1709, aged 16 (he was therefore born about 1693); and graduated Bachelor of Arts and Master of Arts, in course, and afterwards Bachelor of Medicine and Doctor

of Medicine. He became a Fellow of the Royal College
of Physicians of London June 25, 1724, and Censor in
1726-7; and died May 23, 1727, unmarried. His will,
dated May 19, and proved July 27, 1727, left his whole
estate, both real and personal, with the exception of a
single legacy of £50, to his sister Elizabeth, then un-
married—coinciding with the tradition that William
Diodate, on returning to England after the death of his
brother John, when his father also had died, found himself
disinherited. This sister afterwards married a gentleman
of the name of Scarlett—probably Anthony S., whose will,
dated May 8, 1750, and proved March 1, 1757, by his relict
Elizabeth, left his entire estate to her, "as a testimony of
the great love and most tender affection which" he had
"for the best of wives." She died in 1768, her will having
been proved April 13 of that year, with a codicil which
she added Feb. 22 of the same year, in which the principal
legacies are to "the children of" her "niece Elizabeth
Johnson deceased, late wife of the Rev. Mr. Stephen
Johnson of Lime, in Connecticut in New England."
This record brings us back to our subject, William
Diodate, the only other child of John Diodati by his
Morton-marriage, whose daughter, as appears from his
will in the New Haven records, was that Elizabeth
Johnson, thus named in the will of her aunt Scarlett.

It only remains to say that the son-in-law of William
Diodate, Stephen Johnson, named in his will, a son of
Nathaniel Johnson, Esq., of Newark, New Jersey, by his
wife Sarah Ogden, was not unworthy to transmit the accumulated honors of the Diodati race to his descendants;
for, beside being an honored pastor, for forty years, over a

single church, he was an eminent patriot—perhaps contributing as much as any other one person to bring on the Revolution, by his strong and impassioned articles in opposition to the stamp-act, published in New London papers of the day, through the agency of his parishioner and intimate friend and counsellor John McCurdy, ten years before the actual breaking out of the war; which led to the banding together of the "Sons of Liberty" in organized association, first in Connecticut and afterwards in other colonies; and on the 22d of May, 1775, when the conflict of war had begun, he asked leave of absence from his people in order to accept the appointment of the General Assembly of the colony to be chaplain to the regiment of Col. Parsons, which was afterwards present at the battle of Bunker Hill. The historian Bancroft says: "Of that venerable band who nursed the flame of piety and civil freedom, none did better service than the American-born Stephen Johnson, the sincere and fervid pastor of the First Church of Lyme."" His descendants, also, proved worthy of their inheritance: Diodate Johnson, his son, a young clergyman cut off in his twenty-eighth year, was "eminent for genius, learning and piety;" and his daughter Sarah, who became the wife of John Griswold, son of the first Governor Griswold of Connecticut by his wife Ursula Wolcott, handed down the precious legacy of "blood that tells," in cultured manners, warm affections, noble aspirations, and quick intelligence, betokening, in the case of some of the generations which have succeeded, in no doubtful manner, the hereditary influence of old Italian genius and temperament.

NOTES.

—·· ◆◆◆——

[1] Proceedings of the City of New Haven in the Removal of Monuments from its Ancient Burying Ground, etc., New Haven, 1822, p. 26.

[2] The inscription on her gravestone reads as follows: "In memory of Mrs. Sarah Diodate, relict of Mr. William Diodate, who departed this life the 25th April, 1764, in the 75th year of her age."

[3] In 1833 this piece of plate was melted up, with others, to make new cups, on one of which Mrs. Diodate's gift is recorded as follows, in connection with that of another: "Presented to the First Church in New Haven by FRANCES BROWN, Rev. Mr. Noyes being pastor, AND BY Mrs. Sarah Diodate in 1762. Made anew in 1833."

[4] Rev. Andrew Le Mercier came to this country in 1715, and became the pastor of a French Protestant church in Boston. "In 1732 he published a minute and interesting history of the Geneva Church, in five books, 12mo., 200 pages; also, in the same volume, 'A Geographical and Political Account of the Republick of Geneva,' 76 pages." See New Engl. Hist. and Geneal. Register, xiii. 315–24.

[5] The record stands thus: "William Diodate's Book, August 24, 1728. The owners of this Bible have been: 1. Mr. John Wicker; 2. Alderman Cranne of London, who married his only child; 3. John Morton, Esquire, her second husband; 4. Mr. John Diodate, who married his eldest daughter; 5. John Diodate, M. D., his eldest son; 6. Elizabeth Diodate, his sister, and by her given 7. to William Diodate, her brother, Aug. yᵉ 24, 1728, and by him given to his dear and only child [so far in W. D.'s handwriting]; 8. Elizabeth Diodate, who was married July 26, 1744, to Mr. Stephen Johnston of Newark in Est Jersie, etc. etc."

[6] A genealogical chart of all the ramifications of the family, of which we are informed, beginning with Cornelia, is appended to this paper. In one of the family-documents, entitled "Notes Généalogiques tirées des Archives de M.

Rilliet Neckar, Commissaire Général," three other names are found before that of Arrigo in our chart, namely : Ugolino, d. at Lucca 1150 ; Cristoforo, d. at L. 1191 ; Uberto, d. at L. 1234 ; and Jacopo—who is called " Dominus de Barga"—d. at L. 1304 ; while the name of Cornelio is omitted, apparently by accident. But we learn, by a letter from Mr. Theodore Diodati of Geneva, that his grandfather always considered the Diodatis of Barga as forming a separate branch ; and the dates above given seem not likely to belong to successive generations: so that we have here, probably, an ill-considered attempt to trace the origin of the family from a still higher antiquity. If Schotel (pp. 12-13) is right in his understanding of Baronius, one of the name held the papal chair from 614 to 617, as the successor of Boniface 4th. For completeness, we may add that Schotel (p. 12) refers to " L'État de Provence, dans sa noblesse," Paris, 1693, iii, 28 ; Cæsar Nostradamus, "Histoire de Provence," Lion, 1614, p. 697; and Mich. Baudier, "Hist. du Maréchal de Toiras," Paris, 1644, as showing that some have believed the Diodatis to be not originally Italian, but of French extraction. But the last of these references—which is the only one we have been able to follow up— has given us nothing pertinent to the subject ; nor do Schotel's quotations, on pp. 97-8, from the first two of the works referred to, seem to support his statement. Coreglia and Barga are both small castle-towns, with dependent territories, on the torrent-worn declivity of the Appenines, four miles (Italian) apart, and about twenty miles north of Lucca : s. Repetti, Dizion. Geogr. Fisico Storico della Toscana, i. 273 ff., 796 ff.

All the names and dates of our chart have the authority of family-records, but there is reason to fear that the order of names belonging to a single generation may not, in all cases, have been correctly given, though we have aimed at the utmost precision possible.

[7] Histoire des Républiques Italiennes du Moyen Age, iv. 164.

[8] Hist. d. Répubbl. Ital., xii. 4 ff.

[9] De Hudé, p. 10.

[10] In J. B. Rietstap's Armorial Général, Gonda, 1861, we find the following : " DEODATI—Lucques, Suisse, Neerl. Part; au 1 de gu, un lion d'or; au 2 fasce d'or et de gu.; C; le lion, iss.; D; Deus dedit." A family-document preserved at Geneva informs us with respect to Giulio Diodati, grandson of a brother of that Michele who entertained the Emperor Charles in his palace, that " L'Empereur [Ferdinand 2d] pour reconnoitre les grands et importants services qu'il lui avait rendûs, le fit comte, et que, si'l ne se marioit pas, le titre passeroit à ses collateraux, et permit à la famille d'augmenter leurs armes d'une double aigle Impériale "—forming, accordingly, the background and crest in a blazon of the Diodati arms which is attached to a Patent of

Joseph 2d, presently to be mentioned. An older coat, identical with Rietstap's description, except that the left of the shield, in heraldic language, is barry of six pieces, instead of fesse or and gules, is still to be seen, in stone, over the door of a palace in Lucca, now known as the Orsetti, which must, therefore, have been the old home of the family; and the point of difference here indicated may show, perhaps, what was the quartering granted by Charles 5th. The family in Geneva, at the present time, use the arms which are engraved for our frontispiece—substantially the same with the blazon in the Patent of Joseph 2d, though slightly differing from that in the execution of details, and believed by the family to be so far more correct: the terms of the grant to Giulio Diodati by Ferdinand 2d would seem to authorize any branch of the family to use the imperial double eagle as part of their arms.

[11] Schotel, p. 125.

[12] De Budé, p. 16; and Schotel, p. 7. The former erroneously gives Calandrini as the maiden-name of the wife of this Nicolò.

[13] Schotel (p. 104) gives this inscription as follows:

"D. O. M.

Et memoriæ æternæ Julii Diodati Patricii Lucensis qui bellicæ gloriæ natus Ferdinando ii. Imperatore per omnes militiæ gradus inter summos Copiarum Præfectos adscitus Luzenensi prælio in quo Gustavus Sueciæ Rex interfectus est dextero lateri præfuit fideque ac virtute singulari claras urbes Lincium et Ratisbonam ex hostibus recepit.

Sexies ferreá glande ictus semel cœlesti prodigio servatus in parvo Carmelitarum habitu globi impetu fracto demum ad recipiendam Moguntiam a Cæsare missus ictu parvi tormenti decessit.

In ipso victoriæ suæ spectaculo gentis patriæ militiæ decus anno 1635 26 Julii ætatis xli.

Octavius una cum fratre Johanne Equite Hierosolimitano Venetiarum Priore fratre amantissimo cum lacrymis poni supremis tabulis jussit. Nicolaus Deodatus Octavii hæres et curatores testamentarii posuerunt Anno Domini 1671."

In the same church is a chapel of the Diodatis, with the following inscription, as given by Schotel (pp. 104-5):

"D. O. M.

Aram in honorem S. Nicolai Tolentinati a nobili Deodatorum familiá erectam, in quá Hieronimus Deodatus, Michaelis filius, stipe monachis S. Augustini legatá testamento per Jacobum de Carolis excepto anno 1512, sacrum alternis diebus defunctis familiæ piaculo solvendis fieri in perpetuum jussit. Octavius Deodatus, Nicolai filius, lapideo opere ornari, jussitque in eá quotidie sacramenti hostiam immolari suis Hilaríæque uxoris et Julii fratris manibus expiandis, nec non quotannis septimo Calendas Augusti sacrum majus ac triginta minora in perpetuum fieri, fundo iisdem monachis legato, qui onus susceperunt Cal. Martii 1670. Tabulis publicis a Paulino de Carolis eâ de re confectis."

[14] Hist. d. Republ. Ital., xvi. 207 ff., 220, 274, 284 ff.

[15] Letter of Rev. L. W. Bacon, dated Feb. 18, 1875. A beautiful photographed copy of this Patent has since been received from Geneva, through Mr. Bacon's kindness. The substance of it is that, in consideration of the ancient nobility of the Diodati family, and its distinguished public services and dignities, both in the old Italian home and in foreign lands, as well as of the recognition of their high position by the King of France in 1719, and in consideration, further, of high personal distinction and claims of merit of a certain John Diodati, great-great-great-grandson of Pompeio, grandson of Gabriel, and son of Abraham, the Emperor confers a countship of the empire with the amplest dignities and privileges, upon him and upon all his children and direct descendants, being legitimate, of both sexes. It is dated at Vienna, Oct. 4, 1783. This John is the same who has been named above (p. 14) as the last in the line of direct descent from Pompeio. Attached to this Patent is a blazon of the Diodati arms, described as follows : " Ut autem eo luculentius de collatâ hac Sacri Romani Imperii Comitatis dignitate omni posteritati constet, non solum antiqua nobilitatis ejus insignia clementer laudamus et approbamus, ac quatenus opus est de novo concedimus, sed ea quoque novis accessionibus exornata sequentem in modum omni posthac tempore gestanda ac ferenda benigne elargimur. Scutum videlicet militare erectum aquilae bicipiti nigrae coronatae, expansis alis et exsertis linguis rubeis. Impositum, in duas partes aequales perpendiculariter sectum, in cujus parte dextrâ rubeâ leo aureus exsertâ linguâ rubeâ caudâque a tergo projectâ extrorsum versus conspicitur, sinistra vero auro et rubeo colore in sex partes aequales divisa est : telamones ex utrâque parte sunt leones aurei capitibus extrorsum versis, linguis rubeis exsertis, caudisque a tergo projectis ; et tandem in calce scuti sequens symbolum Deus Dedit in schedulâ inscriptitiâ literis nigris legitur: prout haec omnia propriis suis coloribus in medio hujus Nostri Caesarei diplomatis accuratius depicta sunt."

[16] The Poetical Works of John Milton, ed. . . . , by David Masson, ii. 324.

[17] David Masson's Life of John Milton, ii. 81, note.

[18] Ibid., i. 80.

[19] Charles Symmons's Prose Works of John Milton, vi. 117.

[20] De Budé, pp. 164-5. Richard Simon, on the other hand, thought Diodati's translation too periphrastic, and more definite on the side of his own

theological opinions than the original text. But Diodati seems to have spared no labor to perfect his work in successive editions: the younger Buxtorf wrote of him that his authority as an interpreter of Scripture had great weight, inasmuch as he was chiefly occupied, all his life, " in examinando sensu textus sacri, atque Bibliis vertendis :" s. Schotel, p. 21 ; and the English editor of his Annotations, in 1651, said that " in polishing and perfecting them, in severall editions, he hath laboured ever since" he first finished them.

²¹ Chalmers' Biogr. Dict., xii. 107.

²² Brandt, iii. 79.

²³ Brandt, iii. 116.

²⁴ Brandt, iii. 253.

²⁵ Brandt, iii. 267.

²⁶ Brandt, iii. 281. A cruel witticism, even, is attributed to Diodati, on the occasion of the execution of Barneveldt—that the canons of Dort had been the death of him : but such words seem very unlikely to have come from his lips.

²⁷ Masson's Life of Milton, i. 778.

²⁸ Ibid.

²⁹ A grand-daughter of the Francesco B. who conspired to liberate the republics of Tuscany in 1546, and sacrificed his life to his patriotism : s. Hist. d. Républ. Ital., xvi. 128 ff., and Schotel, pp. 11-12.

She had a sister Renée—so named by the celebrated Renée Duchess of Ferrara, who was her godmother—who married, first, Cesar Balbani, and, afterwards, Theodore Agrippa d'Aubigné, the grandfather of Françoise d'Aubigné Marchioness de Maintenon: s. Schotel, pp. 12, 92. Jean Jacques Burlamaqui, author of the well-known " Principes de la Loi Naturelle et Politique," was a cousin of the wife of Rev. John Diodati, and appears to have married a sister of his. The Burlamaquis were " one of those noble families of Lucca," says Nugent, the English translator of that work, " which, on their embracing the Protestant religion, were obliged, about two centuries ago, to take shelter in Geneva :" between them and the Diodatis there were several intermarriages. A touchingly simple narrative of dangers and escapes, privations and succors, experienced by the family of Michel Burlamaqui, father of Madeleine and Renée, in passing from Italy, by the way of France, to their final resting-place in Geneva, which was written by Renée in Geneva, is given by Schotel (pp. 85-95) from family-archives. At one time they were sheltered in a palace of the Duchess of Ferrara at Montargis, where Renée was born. Again, being in Paris during the massacre of St. Bartholomew, the very palace of the Duke of Guise, through the intervention of some Roman Catholic relatives, became their place of refuge. Afterwards, in the house of M. de Bouillon, temptations to a denial of their faith, by conformity to the usages of the old church, beset them ; but from these, too, they escaped unscathed. Finally, after years of moving from place to place, they reached Geneva, stripped of all earthly goods, but rich in the treasure of a good conscience, and "extremely joyous and consoled."

[30] De Hudé, p. 298. At our request, through the intervention of missionary-friends, a search has been lately made for this monument, in the English, French and Dutch cemeteries at Surat, but without success : the climate, time and neglect would seem to have destroyed all traces of it.

[31] Hist. of the United States, v. 320. Our country's indebtedness to Johnson in the matter of resistance to the stamp-act is fully recognized by Bancroft, as, for instance, in his Hist., v. 353, where he calls him "the incomparable Stephen Johnson of Lyme ;" and long ago, by Gordon in his Hist. of the Rise, Progress and Establishment of the Independence of the United States, i. 166 ff.

www.ingramcontent.com/pod-product-compliance
Lightning Source LLC
Chambersburg PA
CBHW030914260626
47169CB00008B/2839